MY AMERICA

Five Smooth Stones

Hope's Revolutionary War Diary

· Book One ·

by Kristiana Gregory

Scholastic Inc. New York

Philadelphia, Pennsylvania
1776

Monday, the 15th of January

'Tis snowing again. The wind is fierce. Mother and I hurried outside to close the shutters. Our feet got wet so we've hung our stockings by the fire to dry. Oh, how the wool stinks!

Mother has gone upstairs to bed, but said I may stay by the hearth to write in my diary. I shall hurry, as the light is dim and the room is growing cold.

Oh, the heartache of today. . . .

It began as we were eating our porridge. I scraped ice off the window to look out, to see what sort of day it might be. Coming down the street was a soldier on horseback, mayhaps an

 3

officer, from the silver on his coat. Behind him, four men carried a stretcher. As it passed, we were shocked to see that on it lay our dear neighbor, Mr. Quinn. . . . Oh, his face . . . the blood.

Mother grabbed her shawl from the hook and called for me to bring clean rags. I lay down my spoon, eager to help. When I followed her outside, I saw that Mr. Quinn's wounds had bled onto the stones.

To bed now. . . .

Tuesday, the 16th of January

Missed school yesterday, helping Mother help Mrs. Quinn. Her poor husband! He was guarding cannons and gunpowder for General Washington when there was an accident. An explosion cut him open in such a way we fear he may not live through the night.

Mrs. Quinn wept in Mother's arms. She is a bride of just two years. They have worked hard at their new trade: sewing drapes, chair covers, and flags for ships. But now a little sign in their window reads NOT OPEN.

Her house is 'round the corner from ours and is also red brick. It is two stories high with an attic and a cellar. We share a low stone wall out back. This opens up to a courtyard where there is a well for us to share with other neighbors.

'Tis my task now to fill her water pitchers, something I am most pleased to do. Many times this morning and afternoon, I dropped the bucket down, let it sink, then pulled it up by its soggy rope. Chips of ice floated on top. My fingers were red and numb from the cold water, but I shall complain not. A girl of nine years such as myself should do for others without tears of her own.

Wednesday, the 17th of January

Before school this morning, I brought water to Mrs. Quinn.

"Thank ye, Hope," she said. She pointed to the pot heating in the fireplace. With the hem of my apron, I pulled the pot toward me, then poured in the fresh water. Turning to leave, I noticed the bed.

A lace curtain hung around it from the canopy, so I could see just a shadow of her husband. He lay on the pillows, his head bandaged. Oh, I was heartsore to hear his wife's tears as she so tenderly spoke to him. He tried to answer, but only a terrible sound came from his throat.

I walked to school along the stepping-stones, grieving for our neighbor. Lost in thought, I slipped and fell into the snow. All morning I suffered in class from wet stockings and wet petticoats. But my suffering was not as great as my friend Polly's. Hers I shall tell of to-morrow.

Thursday, the 18th of January

The cat broke my quill. I found her carrying it in her mouth like a dead bird. 'Twas two days before I earned a ha'penny from Mother to buy another — a tall black crow's feather. For this sum the man in the paper shoppe also gave me a packet of ink-powder he made from oak gall and iron. I mixed it this morning with water, then filled my little jug three inches deep. Fresh ink has a sharp smell.

Now, about Polly . . . Teacher called on her to spell "porcupine." She knew well its meaning, but could not spell it properly.

Teacher sniffed. "Thou art a baby-good-for-nothing," he said. "Class? Who is a baby?"

My voice was silent as the others called out, "Polly Adams!"

Dear Polly was made to walk to the front of the room. Her head was down when Teacher bade her sit on the stool in the corner. "Cast thine eyes forward, baby." He placed a tall hat on her head. 'Twas shaped like a cone, pointing up with the word "dunce" written on it.

Dunce means stupid.

He then hung a sign around her neck. It said BABY-GOOD-FOR-NOTHING.

All day she sat thus. When her eyes met mine, I swallowed hard and cried for her. A dunce is allowed no tears, or a thrashing will follow.

Before bed

Ethan came in at sunset, just as Mother set our soup on the table. He kissed her cheek. At thirteen, he is taller than she is and handsome like our father. He sat on Papa's bench, as he is now the man of our home. This past week, he has been staying in the harbor to help the ship builder carry wood and to earn a few pence. The Delaware River is a short walk from our front door.

"No new ships," he said. Every day Ethan hopes to see a square-rigger sailing upriver from its ocean voyage, home to Philadelphia. We are waiting for Papa, but we know not if he is hurt or captured or . . .

Oh, to think he may have been killed! We speak not of our fear, for we begin to cry. He went to sea the day after Christmas. I cannot write on this page why, because 'tis a secret. We are at war with England, and King George is now our enemy. That is all I may say.

For dessert, I crushed raspberry leaves into Mother's china teapot, then poured in boiling water. With a little honey, 'tis a comforting hot drink when we miss Papa. (English tea shall not touch our lips, for we are Patriots!)

Friday, the 19th of January

There are so many bakers living on our alley that 'tis called Bread Street, though the tiny shoppe next door to us belongs to a wig maker, Mr. Walker. He is a plump little man who walks with a cane.

At the well this morning, I looked up and saw Mrs. Quinn leaning out her bedroom window, shaking her quilt. Some goose feathers escaped the cloth and floated down into my pail.

"Good morning, Hope," she called to me. Her hair was over her shoulders, not yet pinned up under her cap. Pretty is how I think of her, though it seemed she had been crying.

Saturday, the 20th of January

Polly lives three houses from mine so we are often together. This afternoon she and I put on our wool cloaks and walked to the markets on High Street. Mother wanted me to buy cinnamon sticks.

Polly was so quiet that I said, to cheer her, "Let us trade caps." Only then did she look up from her shoes. We set our baskets on the stones to take off our caps. She tied the ribbon under my chin, and I tied hers. "There, Polly," said I. "Thou art my friend forever." I took her arm in mine.

We walked home by way of the docks. The sun was low in the sky, the air cold. A passing gunboat leaned into the wind, her tall white sails as pretty as clouds. I thought of Papa. *Oh, please return to us soon.*

After supper

'Tis snowing. Wind has been beating hard against the house. Mother, Ethan, and I rushed once again to close the shutters, lest our windows break. This put us in darkness, but for a small red glow under the kettle. I write sitting against the warm stones of our hearth. Mother is reading aloud from the *Evening Post*. Methinks Ethan has fallen asleep on the rug.

In a moment, I shall hide my pen behind the flour sack so the cat will not eat it. She watches my hand as if I am holding a bird.

Sunday, the 21st of January

Six days have passed since the accident that hurt Mr. Quinn. When I carried water over before supper, his wife was upstairs kneeling by his bedside. She held his hand. A rector

I know from Christ Church stood reading from a Bible. *Has she no sisters or friends to comfort her?* I wondered. *Why is she always alone?*

As I filled the washbowl, I could see out the window down to the street. Wagons rolled over the snowy cobblestones. A boy in silk breeches hurried by, carrying three wig boxes stacked in his arms. The next sight thrilled me: A yellow dog was running out of a book shoppe, followed by five yellow puppies, followed by a man waving his arms.

I started to laugh but heard the rector clearing his throat at me. He nodded toward Mrs. Quinn. Oh, my shame! She was covering her husband with a blanket . . . covering his lifeless face.

The room was so still, I heard ticking from the downstairs clock.

Tuesday, the 23rd of January

Mr. Quinn was buried in Christ Church Cemetery, one block away. I know not how a grave was made in the frozen earth, but 'twas. Mother, Ethan, and I sat with Mrs. Quinn. All the bakers from our street came, as did Mr. Walker, leaning on his cane and wearing one of his powdered wigs. No one from Mrs. Quinn's family was there. She has sixteen brothers and sisters! They dwell nearby, yet none came.

Widow Quinn, as others now call her, is just four and twenty years. When I curtsied my respects to her, she lay her hand on my cheek and said, "Dear child, thou mayest call me Sarah."

I wanted to ask about her family, but her eyes were so sad, I said naught.

Next day

Mother is unwell. Her face is pale and she eats only the crusts from our day-old bread.

The cat brought me a wiggly mouse this morning. Methinks she wants to make up for my broken quill. I tossed it into the street by its tail (the mouse).

Before bed

Polly helped me wash the bed linens and the rest. After all was hanging to dry here and there through the house, we cooked supper. To the kettle of water, we added an onion, turnips, and a beef bone. I had just set bowls on the table when someone rapped on our door. 'Twas Widow Quinn, holding a bowl of dumplings. From her apron pocket, she took out a small jug of blueberry jam.

"Comfort thy mother with these," she said.

I curtsied. Before I could invite her in from the cold, she had turned toward her own door. I watched the wind pull at her black dress.

Thursday, the 1st of February

Another blizzard. Wind ripped the door off our privy out back. To fix it, Ethan is cutting leather from a pair of boots Papa left behind. These strips will make new hinges for the door. While he worked at the hearth, I brought him a bowl of my soup. He smiled at me. "Thou art a lady, Hope."

Saturday, the 3rd of February

Mother is brave. Though ill, she does not let herself sleep until the last candle is blown out at night. When I ask what ails her, she says, "I shall live."

When Papa was here, he would rise before dawn to bake. A wooden sign hangs over our door, a sign carved by Ethan when he was just ten years old. It reads POTTER'S PIES. A picture cut from wood shows a plump golden tart. All the bakers on our street have signs like this. Hannie's shows rum cakes. The sign at Polly's house shows a loaf of bread. Another has a gingerbread man, and so on.

Mr. Walker came to buy a meat pie for his dinner. I carried it home for him because he must walk with his cane. He pointed to where his wig maker sign used to be, for it blew down in the storm.

Sunday, the 4th of February

Church. We sat with Miss Sarah in her pew, number twelve. One of the places near us was empty. This is where General Washington prays when he is in Philadelphia. But this day, he is in a soldier camp because of the war.

The chapel was so cold our singing made frost in the air. Mother brought a foot warmer filled with coals from our breakfast fire. Warm feet but cold hands! I tried to turn the pages in our hymnal by blowing the corners up and over. But Mother said, "Hush."

A boy named Phillip sat behind me. I know him from school. He kept pulling a strand of my hair that hung down from my cap. When I brushed at his fingers, he pinched my neck. I turned around just as his mother slapped his hand. But moments later, he started again. Pull. Pinch. Slap. All morning!

After church, Phillip made a face at me. I picked up a stone to throw, but Mother stopped me. If Teacher ties that boy to the whipping post, I shall weep not.

Monday, the 5th of February

Ethan does not go to school because he wants to work and live with the ship builder. But Mother wants Ethan to stay with us, to become a baker like Papa. We also need him here to help with repairs and bring wood for the fire. She and I cannot do everything ourselves.

Thus, my terrible day in school without my brother's comfort. . . . This time Polly had tears for me. I am too upset to write of it now.

Next day

"May I stay home to learn?" I begged Mother this morning.

The backs of my hands are cut and red from yesterday's beating. I shall never look into Teacher's eyes, so cruel is he. He called on me for arithmetick, to add sums. This I did well. Then I sat down. He called on me again, this time to subtract sums. Again I did well. On and on. Divide sums. Multiply sums. He called on no one else.

I was nervous about making a mistake, so I said, "Sir, may I stop now?"

"No, thou mayest not."

From the corner of mine eye, I saw Phillip laugh. My heart burned in me. I could feel tears in my throat. *Why is Teacher picking on me?* I thought. *He is just mean.* I feared to burst out crying, so I sat down.

When I would answer no more, he made me hold out my hands. His ruler hit me again and again. He was so angry, his wig slipped over his eyes.

I can say no more.

Wednesday, the 7th of February

School is every day, save Sunday. Mother says I may now stay home Fridays and Saturdays. I hugged her and hugged her. Then I rolled dough for piecrust twice as fast. I uncorked a jug of strawberries. *I shall make the best tarts ever. Papa will be so proud of me*, I thought.

Before bed Mother gently rubbed oil on my hurting hands. She kissed the tops of my fingers. "Thou must be brave, daughter."

All day Ethan helped Mr. Walker fix his sign. It now hangs by new leather hinges, and the carved wig has fresh, white paint.

Friday, the 9th of February

Polly and I went to market this morning. We each carried a basket with fresh tarts, covered with cloth. Our path is short: down Mulberry Street, 'round the corner, past Christ Church, then home along the docks. The streets are icy so we walk carefully. Even the stepping-stones that cross from one side of the street to the other have ice. Oh, I long for spring and warm sunshine.

A man on horseback cried through the streets that a ship has been spotted off the coast. Mayhaps it will sail upriver in a few days. Could it be Papa? He has been away six weeks.

Sunday, the 11th of February

Ethan came to breakfast holding something behind his back. After prayer he set it on the table in front of my plate. 'Tis a little oak box, long and shallow. Inside were my quill and a new packet of ink-powder.

"Now thy pen shall be safe from the cat," he said. I jumped up to hug him, but my brother blushed and turned away.

I shall always treasure his gift. On the lid he had carved my name: HOPE PENNY POTTER. He himself chose my middle name at my birth. He was just four years of age, but he knew it honored William Penn, the Quaker who started our beautiful colony.

Tuesday, the 13th of February

Such excitement. My bed is high in the attic by the chimney, where the bricks are warm. As I folded my nightdress, I could see out the small window. Over the rooftops and toward the river, there were sails. A ship!

Mother and I buttoned our cloaks against the cold wind and hurried with Ethan. We stood by the river with other neighbors. Sailors threw ropes from the ship down to men waiting on the dock. Up close 'twas tall, the deck high up. The masts were now bare, the sails rolled up under the spars. We waited and watched.

Men walked down the plank. Some were dressed in fine silk vests with silver buckles on their shoes. Others were Quakers in plain black coats and hats.

Someone called, "Mrs. Potter?"

We pushed through the crowd toward the voice. The cry of seagulls made it hard to hear. At last, we saw a sailor waving to us. He pointed to the dock. A small crate stood on end, painted with Mother's name. Ethan lifted it to his shoulder, and we walked home. We said naught to one another.

Wednesday, the 14th of February

Ethan pried open the crate with a hammer. He was careful not to splinter the wood. A letter was inside.

Happy Birthday, Nan, from thine English cousins!

That is all it said. Mother left the room. Papa was not on the ship, and this box was not from him. And her birthday was eight months past. Ethan set the lid back on. "Let us wait until the morrow," he said to me.

Wednesday, the 28th day of February

I have been ill a fortnight. Bad cold and cough. My nose drips and drips. For fourteen nights, I slept with Mother to stay warm. She herself is feeling better and said she shall give me a surprise on the morrow.

Thursday, the 29th of February

This morning, Miss Sarah came for tea with a gift wrapped with a red bow. 'Twas a small downy quilt to fit in a cradle. They were talking about a new baby — our new baby. Mother is three months with child! Sometime in August, I shall have a new sister or brother. Words fail me, I am that happy.

Ethan carried the empty crate upstairs to my room. 'Tis under the window where the light is good. Here I sit on my little stool. There is room for mine ink jug and pen, my diary, and mine elbows! Now I can look out at the sky and seagulls for as long as I want. The cat sits beside me, also watching the birds.

As I opened my journal this morning, I remembered that the 29th day of February occurs just once every four years. Teacher said 1776 is a leap year because the number 1776 can be divided by four. I should like a party or some other happy event to celebrate, but no one seems to care.

Here, here — when Polly comes for tea this afternoon, I shall serve us all an extra cookie. We shall have a leap year party after all.

Monday, the 4th of March

Mother says I have true sewing fingers. My sampler is on heavy tammy cloth made from wool and linen, so my needle can poke in and out and up and down with no rips. Blue thread for ABCs, red thread for numbers. I shall save my finest stitch for a proverb.

Polly and I are learning housewifery under the gentle gaze of our mothers. Why must we go to Teacher's class and bear his cold eye upon us?

The front cover of my primer has a drawing

of King George III. Mother says I may ink out his picture. "We are Patriots," she keeps telling us. "We shall serve no king but King Jesus."

Friday, the 8th of March

I sit with a tall candle. Ethan is to bed, and Mother is knitting with her new bone needles from our English cousins. I forgot to write of the doll they sent me. She is dressed as a proper London lady — full petticoats, tiny high-heeled shoes, ruffles at her throat and wrists, and a big feathered hat. I ask Mother if she would sew me a beautiful dress to match my doll's.

She said, "Dost thou want to be like the English?"

Methinks sometimes yes. We were all born in Britain, but sailed to the Colonies when I was a babe in arms. Other family came, too.

The Potters who now live in Valley Forge are our American cousins. I wish we could visit them more, but the road is long and often muddy. Seventeen miles or so, says Ethan. Another uncle sailed over last year with his young wife, a girl of fourteen. They live in Trenton, in the Colony of New Jersey.

Sunday, the 10th of March

Today is Papa's birthday. After church, I baked a ginger cake. Ethan dribbled icing on top, while I added shavings of cinnamon. At the table, we held hands with Mother to pray for Papa's safe return.

We wait.

Friday, the 15th of March

A booklet is being passed around Bread Street. It seems all of Philadelphia has read a copy. We have heard of it since January and at last can read it for ourselves. Before bed, when Ethan, Mother, and I sit near the hearth, we take turns reading aloud. The title is "Common Sense," written by a Patriot named Thomas Paine. It says in simple words why the Colonies must tell King George to leave us alone. Now simple folk such as bakers and wig makers can understand the cause of the Revolution. 'Tis forty-seven pages.

But tonight, Ethan said something that upset us.

"What if Papa has returned to England without us?" he said, looking into the fire. "What if he is no longer a Patriot?"

At his words Mother's eyes filled with tears. I shall write of this later.

Next morning

Ethan thinks Papa is a Tory! Tories are people who love King George and want America to stay an English colony. They are also called Loyalists because of their loyalty to royalty.

"Why dost thou say this, son?" asked Mother. Her eyes pleaded with Ethan. "Thy father is a Patriot, not a Tory!" she cried.

Ethan didn't answer. When he stormed out the front door, I ran to Mother's arms. We know five families who have packed up their homes and sailed back to England. They were dear friends of ours, we had thought.

Monday, the 25th of March

Such wind. Our shutters are pulled closed even during the day. Candles burn fast, so we use an oil lamp. The fumes give me a headache.

Mother is knitting tiny wool leggings for our baby. My sampler has some crooked letters, but I care not. To rip out and sew again makes me tired. 'Tis time to start my proverb. Green thread shall be pretty, mayhaps a cross-stitch.

Friday, the 5th of April

Snow has melted in front of our house, where the sun hits in the morning. On the stone walk, Polly and I marked squares with charcoal so we may play hopscotch. So, too, the children of Hannie the baker. They come every day with fresh sugar cookies to share with us. Then they play tag up and down

Bread Street. Such noise from the seagulls! The birds cry and circle over our heads, waiting for one of us to throw a crumb.

During afternoon tea, I learned more about Quakers and Miss Sarah. She told us about her lost family. . . . Oh, her tears! (And ours.)

Saturday, the 6th of April

I began stitching a proverb, but it had too many words. I ripped out the letters and shall search our Bible for a shorter one.

All day I have thought about Miss Sarah. She is from a large Quaker family. They forbade her to wed the boy she loved, because he was from another church. But Miss Sarah cared not. She ran away with him, and he took her to wife.

As punishment, the Quakers read her out. She may no longer set foot in their meetinghouse. Friends and family are not allowed to talk to her or buy things from her shoppe. Also, Quakers do not support this war or any war. They do not want to return to England, but they will not help the Patriots.

Thus when her husband died, Miss Sarah was left alone, with not even an infant to comfort her. I see now why she is so kind to Polly and me and Hannie's little ones.

Monday, the 15th of April

Ethan made a kite. With his knife, he cut a triangle from yesterday's newspaper. Polly gave him the ribbon from her hair for the kite's tail. We used scraps of string from the rope maker. We ran down to the harbor where the breeze comes straight upriver from the ocean. We ran along Water Street, down alleys to the docks, then home again. Alas, the kite tangled around the chimney of Hannie's bakery and landed on its smoky top. In one puff of flame, it was no more.

I baked a pork pie for our supper. After dishes were washed, I went down to the cellar. Brought up twenty-four little red apples in mine apron. Dropped them into the kettle's boiling water with molasses and cinnamon sticks and cooked them until they were soft. I wanted these for apple tarts, but Mother says I must first spoon out the seeds and stems as well as the skins.

"We cannot sell tarts full of rubbish," she told me. After she left the room, I said, "Oh, bother!"

I started stitching my new proverb:

TRUST IN THE LORD WITH ALL THINE HEART, AND LEAN NOT UNTO THINE OWN UNDERSTANDING. IN ALL THY WAYS ACKNOWLEDGE HIM AND HE SHALL DIRECT THY PATHS.

Next morning

A sad day. Mother says I must give up my room in the attic! We are to take in boarders who will pay for meals and a bed. She says that until Papa returns, she needs a shilling here and there. 'Tis hard for her to rise two hours before dawn to bake like Papa used to.

I am most unhappy about this, but I want to honor Mother. I nailed this notice to our front door: TO BE LET. Then I ran upstairs to be alone.

Oh, my cozy room! I am sitting by the window and looking out toward the harbor. Fog has settled over the rooftops. I can hear the seagulls but not see them. The cat has curled into my lap, purring, as if to comfort me.

Methinks I am selfish. Mother needs my help but, oh, 'tis hard to give up my nest for a stranger.

A family that is returning to England sold us their rooster and five hens for just a ha'penny! Ethan built a little house for them out back, safe from the wind. Now we shall have fresh eggs.

Saturday, the 18th of May

Polly and I walk to the markets every morning after my baking is done. A cloth over my basket keeps the tarts warm as I call out, "One penny! Tarts, one penny!" This is also where we buy meat and flour and things our mothers ask for.

Today we learned something by hearing men talk at market: The Patriots are astir! The Continental Congress wants to write a letter to King George to declare our freedom. But fear is in the air because of the English ships. They are sailing along the coast, ready to attack us. General Washington is marching toward them with our soldiers and guns. Oh, we must be brave!

Monday, the 20th of May

At school, I minded my manners and did what Teacher said. Polly, too. We do not want to wear the dunce hat or be struck. But mine enemy, Phillip, was not so careful. He and another boy played a trick. It made Teacher so angry he called each boy to the whipping post.

Oh, 'twas terrible. Polly and I covered our ears and closed our eyes so we could not hear or see Teacher's switch. I am heartsore to have wished a thrashing on Phillip. 'Twas only a boy's trick, and Teacher deserved the laughs that came from all of us.

Mother calls. . . .

After supper

Ethan smiled when Polly and I told him about today:

When Teacher left the classroom to visit the privy, Phillip and his cousin crawled into the attic. They drilled a small hole in its floor, just above Teacher's desk. When he returned, he began testing us on Latin words, giving no thought that the boys were missing.

As he talked, mine eyes went up to the hole in the ceiling. A rope was slowly coming down . . . down . . . down. I saw a large fish hook on its end. The hook landed in the top of Teacher's white, powdered wig. Mine eyes were wide at what was about to happen. I dared not look at Polly.

Slowly, the rope was pulled up and with it Teacher's wig! He went mad with rage. His own hair was black and oily. He looked up. We heard shoes running from the attic.

Mother says the whipping will teach boys that tricks are not to be played on teachers. I know not what to think. But today I laughed and then had tears for poor Phillip and his cousin.

Tuesday, the 28th of May

A young gentleman named Robert Dean has taken my room. He pays Mother sixpence sterling to also eat breakfast and supper with us. He is a Patriot from Maine, north of the Massachusetts colony. It took him five days by coach to reach Philadelphia, and he was most tumbled and tired when he came to our doorstep.

Mr. Dean says he is to speak at the statehouse in town. Leaders from each colony are coming here to reason together. Mayhaps we will soon be free from King George.

Polly's family has also taken in a gentleman, from New Hampshire. The inns are full!

Wednesday, the 29th of May

'Tis a dreary day. Black clouds hide the sun. The gloom does not bother me as much as what I said to Polly during tea this morning. Our words turned into a quarrel, and in an instant she marched out of our parlor. She slammed our door so hard it rattled the saucers on our table. I am heartsore! What must I do now?

This is what happened: As I was serving the sugar cubes, I noticed her collar was on backward. It is laced, like mine, and stitched by her own fingers. When I showed her the mistake and also that many of the stitches along her shoulder were improper, she said, "Anything else, Mistress?"

I pointed to her blouse where the thread on one of her buttonholes was undone. "Can ye not do these either?" I asked.

Polly stood. Her eyes were moist. "Hope, thou art a miserable girl!" she said.

After she left, Mother came downstairs. She opened her sewing tin, then drew my hand to her. She rolled my wrist over until I saw how my sleeve was torn and that my own buttonhole was coming apart.

"Daughter," she said, "thou must first remove the log from your own eye before removing the splinter from your neighbor's."

Thursday, the 30th of May

After supper yesterday, I covered a bowl of stewed figs and took them to Polly's. When

I rapped on the door, her little brother answered.

"I do not like figs," he said after peeking under the cloth.

"Please, wilt thou tell Polly I am here?"

"Polly!" he called upstairs. Then he ran outside to play.

I stood on the step for some time. An older brother arrived with an armload of wood for the kitchen. Another brother came out with a lantern and hurried down the street. I did not see Polly, nor her mother. At last, I turned to leave.

Now I am in my nightdress, ready for bed. My heart is heavy. There have been days that Polly and I did not see each other, but never because of anger.

Monday, the 3rd of June

The heat is early this year, so our downstairs windows are propped open. For two days Polly spoke not. I saw her at market, but she turned away when I called after her.

On the third day, I wrote her a letter, slipped it under her door, and ran back home. This is what it said: *Dear Polly, Please be my friend. I am sorry my words hurt you. My collar has mistakes, too. Love, Hope.*

It was early afternoon when she looked in our open window and set her elbows on the sill. "Hello?" she called.

"Hello!" I hurried over. Her hand reached for mine. She said, "'Tis a fine day for a walk. Wilt thou come with me to see the new ship in the harbor?"

"Yes, Polly, I will."

The tall ship was being unloaded with barrels

and crates and sacks. We watched her sailors swab the decks. Then we took crusts of bread from our apron pockets and threw them to the seagulls. The noise! They shrieked and swooped.

Oh, 'twas good to be with Polly, once again whispering our secrets. I am overjoyed that she has forgiven me. I am trying hard to be kind, not to find faults. Mother says that if I look first at my own ragged edges, I will not have time to see them in others.

Tuesday, the 11th of June

The days are hot. Now we open all our windows to the breeze. The cat sleeps on the sill.

I want to do more to help Mother. She is tired and very big. Three more months till she births our baby! Dear Mother.

This morning, I swept Mr. Dean's room.

There was dried mud all over from his boots. I dropped his soiled clothes into a basket to wash. But before carrying it downstairs, I leaned out the window (my window!). Oh, such cool air up here. Seagulls perch on the rooftops as if they, too, watch the harbor. The river was busy. Little boats, barges, a tall ship in full sail . . .

Suddenly, I felt heartsore.

Papa has been gone more than five months. What if Ethan's words are true? What if our father has turned his coat and moved back to England?

I cannot bear the thought.

Friday, the 14th of June

School is closed. Ethan came to tell us that Teacher left in a hurry, some say from illness.

Polly and I looked at each other over our samplers. Without missing a stitch we smiled.

The little garden we planted with Miss Sarah is greening. Soon we shall have lettuce and strawberries and other things, I forget what. This evening, Polly and I saw fireflies in the yard. They were like tiny candles flicking on and off.

Friday, the 28th of June

A fortnight since I have written. Oh, the heat! Poor Mother is slow and light-headed. To be near the fireplace makes her faint, so I am cooking. Yes, I can make a pretty tart. Soup is easy. But bread? Soggy lumps, that is what my loaves look like. And my dumplings are flat as coins. So now we shop at Hannie's.

Miss Sarah is over every afternoon to bathe

Mother's swollen feet in cool water. She cooks our supper. I set plates and spoons on the table. Then she and Mr. Dean eat with us. They look not at each other, yet they chit and chat like two birds on a bench.

Tonight, I learned that Mr. Dean is a Quaker. His family read him out because he wants to help the Patriots.

"Thou must be lonely," said Miss Sarah.

He answered not. But some moments later he told us that he met two men who call themselves Free Quakers. They want to start a meetinghouse for those who have been read out.

"We love God," he said, "but we also love America. We will fight to keep the English away."

Methinks I saw a sparkle in Miss Sarah's eye.

Saturday, the 29th of June

'Tis too hot to wear petticoats and too hot for my cap. Polly and I waded in the cool water of Dock Creek. It curls through town toward the river. In the shallow part of the harbor, we saw a boy swimming. But when he came out dripping wet, he told us he knows not how to swim!

I said, "Then why didst thou not drown?"

He proudly showed us eight large corks he had sewn into his waistcoat. There were brass rings down the front, tied with rope instead of buttons. This outfit he sewed himself from white sailcloth.

Just then his master, the sail maker, marched down the dock toward us. He grabbed the boy by his ear. "Lazy dog," he yelled. "Get thee back to work!"

On our way home, Polly and I giggled. We liked this clever boy.

Oh, she finished her sampler. Her proverb is the same as mine!

Sunday, the 30th of June

Ethan is glum. He sat in church like a stone.

"Art thou ill?" I asked him at supper.

"No," he said. Then he left the table, his soup and bread uneaten. He went out the door. Mother called his name, but he answered not.

Polly and I sometimes walk up Mulberry to Seventh Street. The lady of the house on the corner asked us to bring fresh strawberry tarts on the morrow. Like us, she has a gentleman boarder. He is from Virginia and loves strawberries.

Before bed

After supper, I walked barefoot along the river in search of a cool breeze. The shore is marshy, but the mud felt good between my toes. To my surprise, someone jumped off a nearby dock and swam toward me. Once again 'twas the boy in his floating waistcoat.

"Hello, lass!" he shouted. "Thou art a pretty sight this evening."

Before I could answer, he rolled onto his back and with splashing arms and kicks swam back to the dock. When I was walking home, I saw the boy's master, the sail maker. He was heading toward the river, his face red with anger.

Mayhaps 'tis too hot for a boy to work all day long.

Monday, the 1st of July

When I swept Mr. Dean's room, I found an odd thing. Five stones were lined up along the windowsill. *Dost he plan to drop them on someone's head?* I thought.

I left the stones, but propped the window all the way open for air. A seagull flew from the ledge as I did so. 'Tis as hot outside as in, and hotter still in this upper room. In winter, I wish it were warm, but in summer I wish for cold. Methinks 'tis a bad habit to want what I cannot have. I must learn to be content.

After supper

Rained all morning. When the sun came out, the air was as hot as steam.

The heat does not go away at night. Mother and I sleep down in the cellar where 'tis cooler. I made her a soft bed from quilts. We cannot leave the doors open lest squirrels and other animals come in. The cat stays out to roam around in the dark. Poor Mother is suffering this summer. She complains not, but I see the heat in her face. She ate her plums and milk on the front step during supper. Hannie's little daughters brought over a fresh loaf of rye'n'Injun. One penny is all they asked for. At the table Mr. Dean sliced the bread.

"Excuse me, please," I said to him. "Art thou to throw stones at our neighbors, sir?"

He laughed, then told us what his five stones were for. But my candle is low. . . .

Tuesday, the 2nd of July

Ethan is more quiet than ever. This evening, he kissed Mother's hand when he came in, but said naught.

"Hello, Hope Penny." That is all he said to me. He tore off a chunk of bread and grabbed a peach from our bowl on the table. He still works for the ship builder, but does not yet dwell with him.

I am heartsore to see him thus. He smiled only when Polly came up the step. Then he was gone.

At night, fireflies swirl through our dark garden. Their tiny lights are here, then there. Hannie's children think they are fairies come to watch over us.

Later

Mr. Dean said men in the Continental Congress are meeting all day long. They talk and argue about the letter to King George. The leaders say that standing up to England is like David standing up to Goliath. I know the story.

Long ago in a land far away, there lived a shepherd boy named David. When the giant, Goliath, wanted to kill him, he took five smooth stones from the river and put them in his pouch. This giant stood nine feet, nine inches. But David told him he was not afraid, because God would help him. David then killed Goliath with his sling and one stone.

Mr. Dean said that when he walked home from the meeting the other day, he sat by the creek. He removed his shoes to cool off. From the water he picked up five smooth stones.

"They remind me to be brave and to trust God," he told us. "If David could slay the giant, we can say no to the king."

Wednesday, the 3rd of July

I must tell about the plump old gentleman. This morning, he bought a berry tart from me, then tucked it into his waistcoat pocket to eat later. (It stained the light blue satin purple!) He is shiny on top but for some white hair hanging over his ears. No wig.

From his other pocket, he pulled out his coin purse. When he put a silver shilling into my palm, I could not speak for the surprise of it. A shilling is worth twelve pence!

"Thou art too kind, sir," I called out to him, as he stepped into a coach.

Mr. Dean passed by just then, while my hand was still open with the coin. "Dost thou not know?" he said. "'Tis Mr. Benjamin Franklin. He is the eldest speaker at the meetings, and the wisest."

Methinks Mr. Franklin is the dearest man I

have ever met. Mother said the shilling is mine to keep. I have tucked it into the little oak chest Ethan made for me.

'Tis so hot, men in the Congress are going mad. In front of the statehouse, Polly and I saw two of them fall out a door. They were hitting each other with their fists. At supper, Mr. Dean told us that tempers are high, and the meetings are filled with shouts.

Before bed

'Tis hard to write in this heat. 'Tis hard to be cheerful. 'Tis hard to clean and to bake. But I must help Mother.

We have beautiful squash and green beans growing out back. Strawberries are plentiful. Polly and I have been taking fresh tarts every morning to the gentleman from Virginia. We have not seen him, for he stays in his room.

The lady said he is writing the letter to King George. Hour after hour, in the hot upstairs all by himself. The men at the statehouse are waiting for him to finish.

She said this letter is to be called the Declaration of Independence.

Thursday, the 4th of July

Hot. I fan Mother with the newspaper to help her cool off. Her neck and face are wet from the heat. Fanning just moves the hot air 'round. It does not ease our suffering.

This morning before breakfast, Ethan was reading "Common Sense." I stepped out for the privy, then came back in, but he was gone. The booklet was in the fire, flames curling over its pages. Oh, what is it that troubles my brother?

A horseman rode through town, crying out

the news: Ten thousand British soldiers have landed in New York! They are camped on Staten Island. Mother says they may take our city next. I am sick with worry. What shall we do without Papa to protect us? New York is just one day's ride from us.

Before bed

Mr. Dean came in moments ago from his meeting. I set out a bowl of soup for him, and brown bread, three slices with fresh butter. He was too excited to eat right away.

" 'Tis finished," he told us. "The letter has been written. And at long last the leaders agreed to sign it and ship it to King George." Mr. Dean said the printer John Dunlap is working all night long. He will make copies so people can read it for themselves.

I ran to Miss Sarah's to give her the good

news. She grabbed a clean white apron from her hook, then hurried over. She set to work over our fire, to make sweet biscuits and tea for us all. When she poured Mr. Dean's cup, he smiled up at her. It was the first time I had ever seen Miss Sarah blush.

"What are we to do now?" I asked him. "The king will rage and send more soldiers."

"'Tis true," he said. "More Redcoats will come. We must be brave and trust God."

Friday, the 5th of July

Our hens give plenty of eggs, but they are as small as my thumb. There were not enough for pancakes this morning, so I made porridge.

While we were eating breakfast, Phillip rapped on our door. Under his arm was a bundle of papers, printed last night by his neighbor

John Dunlap. I wanted to see for myself the letter to King George. Having not a coin, I paid Phillip with a small chicken pie, then sent him on his way. Mother scolded because I did not invite him in.

After washing the dishes, she and I sat out back on a blanket, in the shade of our tall house. Miss Sarah kneeled in our garden picking berries into a basket, while I read the letter aloud. Many words were hard to understand, but Mother helped.

We agreed that King George will be furious when he reads this for himself. The letter calls him cruel and unfit to be the ruler of a free people. He will be furious when he also learns that our country has a new name: the United States of America.

No longer will we call ourselves an English colony.

Monday, the 8th of July

Early, just after sunrise, Polly and I carried our baskets up Mulberry to Seventh, then 'round the corner to Wynne Street. At the statehouse, we saw an old bell ringer ready to climb the steeple. He called out for a tart. I lifted the cloth. With his fingers he picked up two, then put them in a pouch strapped across his chest.

"Bells will soon ring," he said, turning for the stairs.

Polly and I knew not what he meant.

After supper

Such a day. As I swept the front stones, some boys ran past our house crying, "Hurry . . . hurry!"

Mother was sitting in the parlor, her feet in

a pan of cool water. When she saw Polly and me looking out the door, she said, "Ye girls run along. I shall be all right."

We followed the crowd through the streets. Men were shouting with excitement. I saw wig makers, cobblers, the tinsmith, and all the bakers from Bread Street. Men from the shipyard were hurrying with their worker boys.

People crowded in the hot sun in front of the statehouse. Soon a man in white stockings and knee breeches stepped out of the brick doorway. His wig was combed into a pigtail, and his tricorn shaded his face. Unrolling a wide piece of paper, he waited until voices were down to whispers. Then he began to read. It was the letter to King George, the Declaration of Independence — the same as Mother and I read a few days ago.

I remember not all of it. 'Twas quite long. Nor did I *hear* every word, because a man in front of me kept sneezing. But there is one part Polly and I recited to each other all afternoon. I shall write of it later. Mother wants to take a walk now that the sun has set.

Before bed

These are the words to King George as Polly and I could remember them:

We hold these truths to be self-evident.
All men are created equal.
Their Creator gives them certain rights.
Among these rights are life, liberty,
and the pursuit of happiness.

The gentleman who read this letter today stopped many times to clear his throat. Someone gave him a tin cup of water, for the heat was fierce. When he finished, a boy sitting below the steeple clapped his hands and cried up to the old bell man, "Now, sir! Ring! Ring!"

The old fellow pulled the rope, and the bell began to ring. The crowd grew wild. All through town, bells rang over and over and over. Somewhere in the distance there was a burst of cannons. Men tore down the royal flags of England and set them on fire. Nearby was a statue of King George riding a horse. Men hammered at it until it fell.

A blacksmith came with a cart to carry it away. He shouted with his fist in the air, "We shall melt down Old George for bullets, then shoot at the Redcoats!"

'Tis late . . . Mother calls for me to blow out my candle.

Tuesday, the 9th of July

I woke this morning to church bells. There is joy throughout Philadelphia, but sorrow in our home. Mother sits in her chair, staring out the window. Mayhaps a pot of tea will cheer her. The air is steamy hot, but I shall brew the kettle anyway, then hurry to Hannie's to buy bread. Mother loves their puffed rolls for breakfast.

After dishes

I cannot write of yesterday without tears. Late last night, I leaned out the window, hoping for cool air. Something was burning in the street. By the light of the flames, I saw it was a large British flag. But some boys were stomping on the fire, trying to save the flag.

"Long live King George!" one of them

cried. 'Twas my brother! I ran out the door in my nightdress and grabbed his sleeve.

"Ethan," I cried. "Why art thou doing this?"

Seeing me he said, "Papa is a Tory and so am I!" Then he and his friends ran toward the harbor, down the dark street.

Mother stood on our step, holding a candle. In the light, I saw that she was crying. Oh, our hearts are heavy, so heavy. Has my brother gone mad? Or is it true about our father? I had thought Papa was on a secret mission for the Patriots. But now I'm not sure.

Polly is here now. Her cheerful face is a comfort to me.

Tuesday, the 16th of July

A week has passed. The shock to Mother was terrible. Ethan is gone, we know not where. Boys whispering in the street say he has joined the Redcoats. I pray not! Mayhaps he is just looking for Papa?

The heat is dreadful, so we have put out our fire and are cooking at Miss Sarah's. This way only one house is hot. We three sleep together on the stone floor of our cellar. Mr. Dean sleeps on a pallet by the front door. I feel safe with him upstairs.

Just before sunset, Mother walked in our garden. From the window, I saw her reach down to pick up a melon. I turned away to put bread on the table, but when I looked back, she was lying on the ground! The plate of bread fell from my hands as I ran outside.

"Mama!" I lifted her head and brushed dirt from her cheek.

She smiled at me. "Daughter, tell Miss Sarah I shall birth this baby any moment. . . ."

Late, near midnight?

My baby sister came just after sunset, in our soft garden, fireflies nearby. Mother cared not for a bed or even a curtain to hide herself. Miss Sarah laid the baby on a blanket and washed her with cold water that I drew up from the well. The poor little thing let out a wail, but we quickly wrapped her and put her in Mother's arms.

We sat in the growing darkness, a quiet joy between us. A window across the alley glowed with candlelight. Above us, stars. We would have stayed thus all night but for the mosquitoes.

Mother named my sister Faith. She has downy red hair.

Saturday, the 20th of July

This morning, Polly and I walked to the river. 'Tis somewhat cooler there, but the truth is, we hoped to see the swimming boy. We sat on a rock where the water laps.

"The boy likes me," I told her. "He says I am pretty."

She looked at me. "What? I am the one he likes. 'Lovely to behold' — those were his words."

"When did he say this?" I asked. It seems that we have each seen the boy on our own. I think he is sweet on me. She thinks the same of herself. We began to quarrel! Soon we were walking home by different paths. Has the terrible heat made us go mad, like those fighting Congressmen?

Methinks we are jealous of each other! But

this boy is just a stranger to us. We know only that he is cheerful and smart. Must we quarrel over him?

Tuesday, the 23rd of July

My sister has a husky cry for a week-old baby. Mother nurses her every two hours in our rocking chair. I am happy to see her smile again.

During breakfast Polly came to the door with a basket of warm biscuits. "'Morning, Hope," she said.

"Good morning!" I said.

And so ended our spat from Saturday.

Thursday, the 1st of August

Three weeks and some days since we have seen Ethan. Mother cannot speak of him without a catch in her throat. Oh, if only I could show him our new sister!

Over our morning porridge, Mother said I may choose the middle name for our baby, as Ethan did for me.

Thinking upon it all afternoon, I told her at supper. "We shall call her Faith Strawberry Potter."

"My darling girl," she said, "a baby cannot be called 'Strawberry.'"

"But Mother, she is pretty and red on top. And she was birthed in our garden!"

Do ye know that Mother laughed for the first time in weeks?

Saturday, the 3rd of August

Showers. We left our shutters open so rain would wash the dust from our windows. With our front and back doors open, a breeze moved through the house. Oh, such sweetness! But when the rain stopped, the air was hot and thick with stink from the gutters. Here is where people sweep rotting food and other waste.

I find little time to write. Mother needs me more than ever. I rise while 'tis still dark, before our rooster crows, to bake over Miss Sarah's fire. First I dress by candlelight, then step outside, 'round the corner to unlatch her door. I stoke the coals into flames. Her oven is made from bricks set inside the wall of her hearth. On her table, I roll the dough that was set out the night before. Fruit from our berry vines and apples saved from last fall — all go into the tarts. By breakfast I am weary.

Sunday, the 11th of August

Chubby Strawberry (this is what I call my sister) is now three weeks old. I love to watch her as she sleeps in her cradle. She looks like a plump little doll with bare feet. 'Tis much too hot for a blanket. And the wool leggings Mother knit will be of no use until autumn.

When my sister wakes, I rock her in my arms for a few minutes, then change her cloth. This is so Mother can finish scrubbing the pots. Then 'tis my turn to work. I start in the attic, sweeping. I go down the stairs with the broom, poking every corner. Then I sweep the parlor, the kitchen, out the front door, over the step, sweeping last the stones down to the gutter. So much dust every day — cobwebs, too.

Finally, Polly comes and to market we go. All this by seven o'clock in the morning!

Afternoon is more work still. My face is always damp from the heat.

Friday, the 16th of August

Polly and I waded at the river's edge. How good the water felt, first on our feet, then when we splashed our faces. We cared not that our sleeves were soaked, as were our hems.

Where is the swimming boy? we asked ourselves (we promised we would not quarrel over him). After an hour or so, when the sun was high, we headed home to finish our chores. On the dock, we passed by the open door of a storage barn. The sail maker was inside, stacking bags of sails along a shelf. He was complaining to a ship's captain that he was tired. No one would help him.

"My boy ran off," he said. "But he was no good anyway — a stupid lad."

But Polly and I know better! Tonight before bed, I shall pray on my knees for this clever boy. He is bright and brave, not stupid. May he find a good family.

Saturday, the 24th of August

Methinks of my brother Ethan every hour. Where is he? Nearly seven weeks he has been gone from us. And Papa ... eight months since he last set his hand on my head. If they were both here, I should not have to work so hard, nor Mother. But 'tis our lot. We must take courage.

Mr. Dean fixed our cellar door. It opens upward to the street. Some boys jumped on it while playing tag, so the latch fell off. I asked Mr. Dean why he does not return north to his colony. A coach leaves once a week for Maine.

"M'family read me out, Hope," he said.

" 'Tis forever." Now that the meetings are over, he has taken a job at the book shoppe, to begin a new life in Philadelphia.

Friday, the 30th of August

Still hot, but nights are cooler. Mosquitoes are so thick near the river that we cannot walk there after supper.

Criers on horseback brought bad news. Some days ago, British ships dropped anchor in the waters off New York — thousands of Redcoats rowed ashore with guns and cannons. They fought General Washington's small army for two days. Newspapers call it the Battle of Long Island.

At breakfast Mr. Dean said there shall be more attacks. King George still wants to rule America. We must prepare to defend ourselves. Or flee.

Flee? But where? When?

I am sick about this. Why did Ethan run away and leave us? He was the man of our home. My stomach hurts, I am so angry with him. If he wears a red coat, will he come at us with a gun — his own family?

Saturday, the 31st of August

This evening for supper, I melted half a pound of butter into Miss Sarah's wide skillet. Then I cracked open eighteen eggs and dropped them one by one into the bubbling butter, beating it all with a spoon 'til yellow. Dropped in crusts of yesterday's bread. Stirred. Added bits of potato left over from this morning. This fed Mother, myself, Mr. Dean, and Miss Sarah. For dessert, peaches sliced over gingerbread, cream on top. I like to cook.

Washing clothes is a bother. So is mending

and stitchery. But Mother said there are things a girl must learn to do, like them or not. She will school me at home now because she needs me here to help. Also, with the Redcoats just one day north, she wants me near her.

Wednesday, the 11th of September

Rain and sleet. Methinks autumn is soon. Frost is coloring the tops of trees orange, yellow, and scarlet. This morning there were crusts of ice on puddles outside.

Ethan gone now for two months. Mother and I speak not of him.

My Chubby Strawberry smiles and kicks her legs when I look into her cradle. Mother and I love to gaze upon her sweet face. Every day we thank God for our baby, as she eases the heartaches we feel for Papa and Ethan.

Friday, the 20th of September

The nights are cool enough for a fire in our hearth. Mr. Dean sleeps in the attic again. At breakfast this morning, he poured cream on his porridge. Then, while lifting his spoon, he said, "Oh, I forgot!"

He reached into his waistcoat pocket. Out came his five stones. One by one he set them in front of my bowl. "These are now thine," he said. "Thou must be brave, Hope. We know not what the morrow shall bring, but Almighty God does."

After this page, I shall blow on the ink for it to dry. I will put my quill in its little chest, safe from the cat. Next to the shilling, I shall lay my new treasures: five smooth stones. I cupped them in my hand and held them to my face. They smell sweet, of willows from the creek.

Sunday, the 22nd of September

In church, the rector told upsetting news. Much of New York City is in flames. Patriots set their own city afire! With it burning, the British shall have to find somewhere else to winter. Mother squeezed my hand across the pew, for our baby was bundled on the bench between us. "Daughter," she whispered, "we must pray for God's wisdom."

Thursday, the 17th of October

An early snowfall. Here I am, once again wishing it were warm! Shall I never learn to be content?

We brought our pumpkins and squash in from the garden. They are stacked in the cellar along the stone walls. Their colors are so cheerful. Also we have three barrels of apples — we gleaned them from an orchard outside town. Methinks if we must flee, our harvest will be enjoyed not by us, but by enemies.

'Tis not fair.

Tuesday, the 22nd of October

Worries keep me awake at night. Has Papa been lost at sea? Where is my brother?

Three bakers from Bread Street fled in the wee hours, we know not where. We woke to find their windows nailed shut, no smoke coming from their chimneys. Hannie and Mr. Walker are still here, as is Polly's family.

Mother paces the floor with Faith in her arms. If only Papa were here to tell us what to do. Or Ethan. (Shall I ever forgive him for deserting us?) I wrote a note to our Potter cousins in Valley Forge: *Have ye room for a baby plus four?*

Friday, the 25th of October

Horsemen rode by our house crying out the news: "General Washington has moved his soldiers north, away from Manhattan Island."

"North!" cried Mother. "Now there is no one between us and the Redcoats. No one to keep them from marching into Philadelphia. We must leave right away."

As Mother poured our breakfast tea, she asked Mr. Dean if he would please hire a coach, big enough to carry us all. "Yes, of course," he said. " 'Tis mine honor and duty to see ye to safety."

Thus we began packing. We found a basket for Faith to sleep in, one we can carry in a hurry. Another basket is for warm clothes for each of us. My diary will fit inside, as will my little oak box. Miss Sarah has prepared a crate of food to last several days.

We busied ourselves until supper. While I set bowls of stew on the table, Mr. Dean told us he talked to a coachman. But 'twas not good news. The coachman's price goes higher each day because so many people are fleeing the city.

Mother and Miss Sarah began searching every purse, pocket, and tin for coins. Between them and Mr. Dean, they found just eleven pence. The coachman says his price is now two shillings — more than double what we have!

Monday, the 28th of October

Late last night, I suddenly sat up in bed. Mother stirred next to me but woke not. I stepped onto the cold floor and went to the hearth where the coals were warm. From my basket I pulled out the box where my treasures are hidden.

Yes! 'Twas still there, my shilling from Mr. Franklin. Why had I forgotten?

Tuesday, the 29th of October

Polly gave us one pence that she had sewn into her hem for safekeeping. Added to our eleven, we now had twelve pence, plus my shilling. The coachman folded his fingers around the coins when we set them in his hand. I cared not for his fat lips and eyes that looked this way and that. *Greedy and overfed*, thought I.

We leave tomorrow. Polly will care for our cat — she took it this morning. I shall miss her (Polly), but trust we shan't be apart for long.

Later

Moments ago a boy in a torn shirt and torn breeches rapped on the door. He handed a note to Mother, then held out his palm for a coin. Alas, we were all spent. I gave him a blueberry tart and offered tea, but he stuffed the tart in his pocket and ran. We had never seen him before.

Mother unfolded the note. As she read it silently, she put her hand over her mouth and sank into a chair.

"What . . . what is it?" we asked. Mother handed the note to me.

I began reading:

Dear Mother, ('twas from Ethan!) *A friend writes this for me, as mine arm is bandaged. I thought to find Papa with the Redcoats, but they put me in chains and have charged me with being a spy. Mother,*

thou must forgive me, please. I was fool-
ish. Thy son, Ethan.

After the color returned to Mother's cheeks, we four sat over tea. Mr. Dean said he has friends who have friends who have friends. They can secretly find where Ethan is held. These friends will ask for his freedom.

"They shall tell the British officers that he is no spy, that he is just a lad of thirteen years, a boy who made a mistake."

At this we took hands and prayed. We asked God to protect Ethan. No one spoke aloud our most terrible fear: spies are punished by hanging. When methinks of my brother sitting in a cold prison, my heart melts. From now on, I shall spend my thoughts toward him on prayer, not anger.

'Tis late. We leave on the morrow, early.

Thursday, the 12th of December
Valley Forge, Pennsylvania

Six weeks have passed since writing last. I am busy watching little ones and helping about. I have no quiet corner to call my own, but I complain not.

We made it safely to our cousins. The road was slow, seventeen miles of bumps and dips. The wheels of our coach rolled over holes filled with brown ice. The driver unloaded our luggage two miles from the farmhouse and said we must walk the rest of the way. It was foggy and wet from sleet. We were so very cold and tired, but he would go no farther.

When he held out his hand for a tip, Mother's eyes grew wide. She said, "Thou hast the nerve of a rooster and a brain no better." She picked up the basket with Faith sleeping in it and turned on her heel.

Next morning, before breakfast

We all have warm beds. Mine is up in the attic with four girl cousins. Already we chit and chat like sisters. Mr. Dean sleeps in the barn with two of my boy cousins — they are small and call him "Uncle" though he is not. They have given up their own bed to Mother and Miss Sarah. My Chubby Strawberry sleeps in a box by the fire. She is nearly five months old!

I cannot say our hearts are merry, but we are not in silence over Ethan. Mother speaks his name without tears. We wait. We are trusting God to protect him and Papa.

Mr. Dean is helping mine uncle about the farm. For the past three days they have been repairing a stone wall that washed apart in the rain at summer's end.

Before bed

Yesterday, I cried from missing Polly. But I am comforted that she has a father, brothers, and some big uncles to protect her family. Another comfort is this: If Ethan should be freed, he would come home, find our house shuttered, but know to call on Polly. Then she would tell him where to find us, she would.

Tuesday, the 17th of December

There is a tiny window up here by my bed. Along the sill, I have lined up my five stones and next to them my little jug. 'Tis so cold at night that by morning I must hold the jug over a candle to thaw the ink. Another matter is the cats — *five* of them. They creep about, upstairs and down, looking for things to eat. Thus I hide my quill in its little box so they shan't mistake it for a bird.

Out the foggy glass, I can see 'tis snowing again. White covers the fields and fence posts. A sleigh drawn by horses just passed by the house and turned up the lane. I hear bells from their collars ringing and jingling.

'Tis peaceful in this valley. And cold! But I am content to let it be so.

Oh, Auntie calls. I must help with dinner. She says that next week I may bake the Christmas pies!

Friday, the 27th of December

Late. I write by a short oil lamp. My four little cousins are tucked into their bed under a thick downy quilt — I can see only the tops of their nightcaps. Tucked under my own blankets are some potatoes from the fireplace to warm the cold sheets. Two gray cats are curled over this warm spot. Their purring makes me want to hurry in beside them. But first I must tell our exciting news:

Today word came from mine uncle in Trenton. In the wee hours of Christmas, General Washington and his army crossed the Delaware River in boats. He marched into the village where the enemy lay sound asleep. They were so groggy our soldiers were able to capture them, most still in their nightshirts. Mother is overjoyed, for at long last, we have won a battle against England! God answers prayer.

I can hear Mother and the others downstairs, laughing and serving up pie. Such a clatter of plates and teacups! How can I go to bed when there is such happiness under our roof?

Alas, I cannot. So I shall snuff out this tiny flame and join them. I know in my heart that Papa and Ethan shall return to us.

Life in America
in 1776

Historical Note

The year 1776 began with the publication of a pamphlet, called "Common Sense," by Thomas Paine. It explained why America no longer wanted to be a British colony, and it was so persuasively written that soon thousands were converted to the Patriots' cause.

In March the British evacuated Boston and sailed for Nova Scotia to plot their attack on New York. Three months later, at the end of June, they made their move and landed in New York Harbor with a huge fleet, signaling their plan to begin a full-scale invasion.

Meanwhile, members of Congress had formed a committee to prepare a Declaration of

Thomas Jefferson writing the Declaration of Independence.

Independence, with Thomas Jefferson selected to write it. While drafting this document, Jefferson, the "gentleman from Virginia," boarded at the home of Jacob Graff in Philadelphia. On July 4, 1776, Congress adopted his draft, and a few days later it was proclaimed on the steps of the state-house. In New York, the Declaration was read to General Washington's troops, followed by a bonfire and men tearing down the equestrian statue of King George III. Thomas Jefferson was to become our nation's third president.

In the following weeks, British general Sir William Howe moved his troops across New York. The Battle of Long Island was fought from August 27–28. On the 29th, the Americans surprised their enemies by having slipped away in the middle of the night.

A peace conference was held a week later on Staten Island, New York, but good will dissolved when General Howe demanded that the Declaration of Independence be torn up. The Americans refused, so the war resumed.

Congress fled Philadelphia on December 12, fearing that the city would soon be invaded as well. Two weeks later, on Christmas night,

The reading of the Declaration of Independence.

George Washington and his troops crossing the Delaware River.

General Washington led a surprise assault on a British camp in Trenton, New Jersey. He and his men crossed the Delaware River in large cargo boats, using poles to push themselves across. The weather was miserably cold with huge chunks of ice floating in their way. Washington captured some one thousand Hessians, who were German soldiers paid by the British to fight on their side. This was a decisive victory for the Patriots, but the Revolutionary War did not end for nearly seven more years.

Benjamin Franklin was seventy years old

when he signed the Declaration of Independence. Soon afterward he sailed to France, where he persuaded French soldiers to come help the American army.

Benjamin Franklin.

The character of Sarah Quinn is modeled after Betsy Ross, who lived in a narrow brick house around the corner from Bread Street. When her husband died from a war accident, she continued to run their upholstery shop.

Betsy Ross along with other seamstresses sewing the first flag of the United States.

Such was her reputation that General George Washington visited her in late May of 1776 and asked her to sew a flag with thirteen stars and thirteen stripes. She did. This was to be our nation's first flag. It was recognized by the Continental Congress on June 14, 1777, the date we now celebrate as Flag Day.

Betsy Ross had sixteen brothers and sisters. When she married a non-Quaker, she was "read out" from her family and meetinghouse. In 1780, eight Quakers from Philadelphia, who had been "read out" for supporting the war, formed their own meeting. They called themselves Free or Fighting Quakers.

The first flag of the United States.

A Quaker meetinghouse.

The brick building they put up is still standing today and is one of the oldest Quaker houses of worship in Philadelphia.

The Pennsylvania statehouse is now called Independence Hall. The bell that rang for so many hours after the Declaration was first read in public is displayed nearby. In the 1800s, it was named the "Liberty Bell" by abolitionists who wanted to end slavery, and it has become an international symbol of freedom.

The Liberty Bell.

About the Author

In researching My America: Five Smooth Stones, Kristiana Gregory wandered the streets of Old Philadelphia and toured historic sites with her teenage sons and other family. Working from maps of 1776, she was able to "see" Hope's neighborhood and the various places where Hope and Polly may have walked and shopped. .

"It was fun to imagine what life was like for a nine-year-old girl in 1776. That year was such an important one in the history of America, especially in Philadelphia. I hope young readers will come away with a sense of *their* own importance. Boys and girls are making history every day just by doing the things they do and by being themselves."

Kristiana Gregory's most recent book with Scholastic is *Cleopatra VII: Daughter of the Nile*, now a Royal Diaries HBO movie. Her other Dear America titles are *The Winter of Red Snow: The Revolutionary War Diary of Abigail Jane Stewart*, also on HBO; *Across the Wide and Lonesome Prairie: The Oregon Trail Diary of Hattie Campbell*; and *The Great Railroad Race: The Diary of Libby West*. Her first book, *Jenny of the Tetons*, won the Golden Kite Award from the Society of Children's Book Writers. Kristiana Gregory lives with her family in Boise, Idaho.

Acknowledgments

Thank you, once again, to Elsie Mullin for help researching schoolchildren in 1776.

Grateful acknowledgment is made for permission to reprint the following:

Cover portrait and frontispiece by Glenn Harrington.

Page 98: Drafting the Declaration of Independence, public domain.

Page 99: The Reading of the Declaration of Independence in Philadelphia. Brown Brothers, Sterling, Pennsylvania.

Page 100: George Washington leads his men across the Delaware River, AP/Wide World Photos.

Page 101 (top): Benjamin Franklin, North Wind Picture Archives, Alfred, Maine.

Page 101 (bottom): Betsy Ross sewing the American flag, Corbis-Bettman.

Page 102 (top): First flag of the United States, North Wind Picture Archives.

Page 102 (bottom): Quaker meetinghouse, North Wind Picture Archives.

Page 103: Liberty Bell, North Wind Picture Archives.

Other books in the My America series

Corey's Underground Railroad Diaries
by Sharon Dennis Wyeth
Book One: Freedom's Wings
Book Two: Flying Free

Elizabeth's Jamestown Colony Diaries
by Patricia Hermes
Book One: Our Strange New Land
Book Two: The Starving Time

Hope's Revolutionary War Diaries
by Kristiana Gregory
Book Two: We Are Patriots

Joshua's Oregon Trail Diaries
by Patricia Hermes
Book One: Westward to Home

Virginia's Civil War Diaries
by Mary Pope Osborne
Book One: My Brother's Keeper
Book Two: After the Rain

While the events described and some of the characters in this
book may be based on actual historical events and real people,
Hope Penny Potter is a fictional character, created by the author,
and her journal is a work of fiction.

Library of Congress Cataloging-in-Publication Data
Gregory, Kristiana.
Five smooth stones: Hope's Diary / by Kristiana Gregory.
p. cm.— (My America)
Summary: In her diary, a young girl writes about her life and the events surrounding the be-
ginning of the American Revolution in Philadelphia in 1776.

ISBN 0-439-14827-8; 0-439-36905-3 (pbk.)

1. Philadelphia (Pa.) —History—Revolution, 1775–1783—Juvenile fiction. [1. Philadelphia (Pa.) —History—Revolution, 1775–1783—Fiction. 2. United States—History—Revolution, 1775–1783—Fiction. 3. Diaries—Fiction.] I. Title. II. Series.

PZ7.G8619 Fi 2001
[Fic] —dc21   00-044662

10 9 8 7 6 5 4 3 2   02 03 04 05

The display type was set in Nicholas Cochin
The text type was set in Goudy
Book design by Elizabeth B. Parisi
Photo research by Zoe Moffitt

Printed in the U.S.A.   23
First paperback edition, May 2002